The
...er Book...

adventure
stories

Also in this series

This collection published 2002 by Walker Books Ltd
87 Vauxhall Walk, London SE11 5HJ

4 6 8 10 9 7 5 3

Text © year of publication individual authors
Illustrations © year of publication individual illustrators
Cover illustration © 2002 Tony Ross

This book has been typeset in Garamond 3

Printed and bound in Great Britain by Creative Print and Design (Wales), Ebbw Vale

British Library Cataloguing in Publication Data:
a catalogue record for this book is
available from the British Library

ISBN 0-7445-6038-1

The
Walker Book of

adventure stories

WALKER BOOKS
AND SUBSIDIARIES

LONDON • BOSTON • SYDNEY

Contents

Emmelina and the Monster

by JUNE CREBBIN
illustrated by TONY ROSS

Once, in a hot and distant land, just outside a village, lived a monster.

It had a long, scaly tail like a serpent. It had the head and body of a cockerel, and it ran so fast, it could catch you in an instant.

But that was not its deadliest power. Oh, no.

Its deadliest power lay in its eyes.

The rule was never, never look into them.

Now, one day, three sisters, knowing nothing of this monster, were travelling towards the village. Their names were Gina, Dina and Emmelina, and their parents had sent them out into the world to seek their fortune.

Gina was a big thumping girl. She liked to eat huge quantities of spaghetti and rich tomato sauce – and thump people.

Dina was tall and vain. She liked to wear beautiful dresses and look at herself in the mirror.

Emmelina was small. She did not eat much (Gina saw to that), or wear fine clothes (Dina saw to that), but she thought a great deal.

As they drew closer to the village, the sisters came to a cornfield. A man was cutting the corn. At least, it looked as if he was cutting. Certainly he held the scythe with its shining blade high in the air. But the blade never fell.

"Lazy fellow!" cried Gina. She tramped across the field and thumped him.

She screamed as her fist struck not skin – but stone.

Then she noticed that all over the field were people who looked as if they were cutting, binding, gathering the corn.

But no one actually moved.

They weren't people, but statues.

"Let's go," said Gina. "I'm ready for my supper."

"But..." began Emmelina. But Gina was already striding up the hill.

On the hillside, they came to a lemon grove. A woman was picking lemons. At least, it looked as if she was picking. Certainly her hand was stretched towards a lemon. But the basket at her feet was empty.

"Oh, goody!" cried Dina. "Lemons! They're so good for my skin. I shall make myself a face-pack straight after supper."

She reached rudely above the woman's head, and touched her arm.

She screamed as her hand met not skin – but stone.

Then she noticed that all over the lemon grove were people who looked as if they were climbing ladders, picking lemons, filling baskets.

But no one actually moved.

They weren't people, but statues.

Gina and Dina were already hurrying on towards the village. For the moment, Emmelina could do nothing but hurry after them.

Close by, the monster stirred in its nest.

When the sisters entered the village, no one was about. They walked right through it without seeing a soul.

But on the other side of the village, they saw a castle, and in front of its great doors, a beautiful woman was speaking to a crowd of people.

"Who is brave enough to rid us of this monster?" she said.

"What monster?" Emmelina asked a boy standing nearby.

Gina and Dina started to head back the way they had come.

"It lives just the other side of the village," said the boy. "You must never, never look into its eyes, or it will turn you to stone."

Gina and Dina stopped.

Then Gina laughed. "We didn't see any monster on our way here!" she said.

"Just be glad it didn't see you first," said a woman. "I've lost a husband."

"We saw workers in the fields and in the lemon grove turned to stone," said Emmelina. "Is that the monster's doing?"

"Yes," said a man. "We cannot harvest our corn or our fruit."

"And if we cannot harvest," said the woman, "we shall starve."

The beautiful woman, who was the Queen,

spoke again. "I will give my castle to anyone who rids us of this monster!"

There's bound to be plenty of food in a castle, thought Gina.

There are bound to be plenty of fine clothes in a castle, thought Dina.

"I'll do it!" they both shouted.

"No, you won't," hissed Gina, and thumped Dina so hard, she knocked her out.

"*I'll* do it," said Gina, pushing her way to the front. "But first I must have food and a good night's rest."

The Queen, overjoyed, welcomed Gina and her sisters into the castle.

Inside the castle, the Queen gave orders for Dina to be taken to the Blue Bedchamber to recover.

Gina and Emmelina were taken to the Great Hall for a splendid supper. Huge plates of pineapple and pepper pizzas, steaming dishes of ravioli and spaghetti, olives, grapes and garlic bread filled the table.

Gina ate heartily, but Emmelina could eat nothing. Though the Queen entreated her to have at least a thin slice of pizza, or a small dish of spaghetti, Emmelina pleaded tiredness and asked to be excused.

A servant showed her to the Red Bedchamber. Crimson velvet curtains hung at the windows. On

the floor was a scarlet carpet, patterned with cherries and plums and strawberries, and on the table by the bed was a gold lamp studded with rubies. Emmelina climbed wearily into the high bed. It was all so beautiful. But what a mess they were in! Poor Dina, knocked out – and Gina...?

How Gina thought she was going to get rid of this monster, Emmelina had no idea. Still, it was very brave of her to offer.

In the Great Hall, Gina reached for another bunch of grapes – and laughed to herself. She had no intention of getting rid of the monster. She would eat her fill and leave under cover of darkness.

Now for my bed.

"Sleep well," said the Queen.

Not likely, thought Gina as a servant showed her into the Green Bedchamber.

She walked briskly up and down the room to keep awake. But the huge meal she had eaten made her sleepy. And the great four-poster bed looked so comfortable.

She sank onto the soft covers – and fell at once into a deep sleep.

The next morning, when Gina woke, she was horrified to find herself still in the castle. Quietly, she opened the door of her bedchamber.

Outside stood a guard. He drew his sword.

"Let me pass!" cried Gina. But the guard took her to the Queen.

"Now," said the Queen. "Is there anything you need before you go?"

"Yes," said Gina. "I need a suit of armour. Send for the blacksmith!"

She thought that while it was being made, she could escape.

"No need," said the Queen. "I'm sure we have one just your size."

A suit of armour was brought. It was exactly right.

Well, thought Gina, nothing can reach me inside this. I might as well slay the monster and claim the castle. It shouldn't take long.

Gina brought down the visor of her helmet over her face.

She clanked out of the castle.

In the lemon grove Gina found nothing. So she clonked along the road to the cornfield.

Close by, the monster watched and waited.

Up and down clunked Gina, round and round.

She wanted to lift up her visor to see better. But she wasn't that stupid.

Presently, at the side of the field, she noticed a vineyard. Bunches of juicy, black grapes hung from every branch. Her mouth watered.

It would only take a minute.

She lifted up her visor, reached for the grapes and – up sprang the monster, lightning zinging from its glittering eyes into Gina's own.

At once, her arm stiffened, her eyes glazed over. Her body turned to stone.

Meanwhile, back at the castle, Emmelina was helping to clear away the breakfast things – and Dina, who had recovered, was looking at herself in a mirror...

How beautiful I am, thought Dina as she tried on one dress after another from the Queen's wardrobe. First, a crimson ball gown stitched with pearls, then a royal blue, shimmering with sequins, then a purple velvet edged with fur.

"Look," she said, when Emmelina came to tell her the sad news that Gina had not returned. "I don't know which suits me best, I look so beautiful in all of them."

Emmelina stared.

"The monster must have turned our sister into stone!" she whispered.

"Well, what did you expect?" said Dina. "They should have sent me." She smirked into the mirror.

The Queen came into the bedchamber. "You're wearing my best ballgown!" she cried.

"Only because I'm going to charm the monster," said Dina quickly.

After all, she thought, he's bound to be a Prince really, turned into a monster by a wicked spell. One kiss from me should do it. Then I'll have this castle – and a Prince to marry.

"Is there anything you need before you go?" asked the Queen.

"Oh, no," said Dina. "All I need is my beauty."

"Remember, never, never—" began the Queen.

"I know," interrupted Dina. She swept out of the castle and down to the lemon grove.

In and out of the trees Dina strutted.

"Here, Princey-Wincey!" she called.

She didn't have long to wait. Ugh! she thought when she caught sight of the monster. He's so ugly! Still, it will be worth it. She closed her eyes.

"Here I am!" she cried. "One kiss from me will set you free!"

She leaned towards him, pouting her lips. She waited. Nothing happened.

So she opened her eyes and – up sprang the monster, lightning zinging from its glittering eyes into Dina's own. At once, her lips set, her eyes froze. Her body turned to stone.

Back at the castle, Emmelina was carefully hanging up the clothes Dina had dropped on the floor...

That night, after Dina had not returned, Emmelina did not sleep. She thought really hard.

"You must never, never look into the monster's eyes," everyone kept saying.

She got out of bed and thought some more. It was so unfair. One glance from the monster... She stopped.

That's it. One glance. That's all it would take.

While it was yet dark, she woke the Queen and explained her plan. "The only thing is," said Emmelina, "I need to borrow something."

"No problem," said the Queen, jumping out of bed.

By daylight, Emmelina was hiding behind a tree at the edge of the cornfield with everything she needed.

She watched for the first sign of the monster. But she was very tired. She told herself stories to keep awake.

Towards midday, when she had just got Cinderella to the ball, the air became very still. She strained her eyes. Something was moving through the corn towards her.

She listened.

Swish, swish. The monster was getting closer.

She drew in her breath and stepped out from behind the tree.

Up sprang the monster, lightning zinging from its glittering eyes into – A MIRROR!

The monster was face to face with itself!

The lightning zinging from its eyes struck the mirror and bounced straight back.

At once, its tail hardened, its eyes dimmed. Its body turned to stone.

Emmelina let out her breath. She looked around. All over the

cornfield workers were cutting, binding, gathering the corn as if they had never stopped.

"Hey!" called a voice. A figure in armour was moving towards her, but she didn't wait for it to catch up.

As she hurried back to the castle, men and women were climbing ladders, picking lemons, filling baskets in the lemon grove.

"Hi!" called another familiar voice, but she didn't even look round.

The Queen was overjoyed to see Emmelina. Soon the news of the stone monster spread.

A great feast was prepared to which everyone – including Gina and Dina – was invited.

And although Emmelina politely refused to accept her reward, she did agree to live in the castle and be the Queen's adviser.

Gina was given a job in the kitchen and Dina in the laundry rooms.

Emmelina lived long and happily. And sometimes, on summer evenings, she would tell the village children the story of the monster and take them down to the cornfield to show them how, in the end, the monster had turned itself to stone.

Kristel Dimond – Timecop

by SAM McBRATNEY
illustrated by MARTIN CHATTERTON

Hi. Kristel Dimond is the name. I'm a Timecop. I proudly wear the uniform of silver and midnight blue.

I was cruising somewhere between Jupiter and Mars when the call came through from my boss, Gusty Monroe.

"Get yourself back here, Dimond, we've got trouble. And when I say trouble, I mean trouble."

I turned to Lefty, my metal companion. "Sounds like a case of double-trouble, Lefty."

"Indeed it does, Inspector Dimond." Lefty is a robot and I call him Lefty because he sits on my left.

I said, "Doesn't it bother you, Gusty, that I'm on my way to Pluto for a skiing holiday?"

It didn't bother him.

"You get back here, Dimond! Somebody has just come through a Timehole – with something that means curtains for the human race."

Naturally, I turned my patrolship around. I belong to the human race and I'm quite fond of it. "Full speed ahead, Lefty. We'd better see what's up."

I docked my ship on the Space Station which orbits the Earth and stepped into a woomzoomtube. Lefty came too. I use him as a kind of butler. The day before yesterday, for example, I sent him out to Pluto to book our skiing holiday. Lefty doesn't get into a foul temper like crusty old Gusty and his body is rustproof. He skis quite well.

On the tube I did some thinking about

Timepirates. They are wild characters who nip into the future, grab some wonderful invention, then bring it back and sell it – before it has been invented. This is highly dangerous and totally illegal, of course.

Ever since Timeholes were discovered, it has been against the law to use them. We can't have people jumping backwards and forwards through time like grasshoppers. I mean, imagine a stone-age lady with a hairdrier…

When I got to Gusty he looked ready for his pension.

"Good morning, Sir."

"Don't 'good morning' me, Dimond, just hang out your ears and listen. Four hundred years from now some brainbox will invent a device that controls the weather, right? No more hurricanes, floods or droughts and the Earth will be a beautiful garden. It's called the Rainmaker."

"Hooray," I said. "What's the problem?"

"The problem is, somebody has been through Timehole Checkpoint Charlie and pinched it. He has it now. And believe me, Dimond, the weather forecast will never be the same again."

"You think he'll use it to make the weather worse?"

"Worse? He could wipe out life on Earth! He could start the next Ice Age tomorrow."

Poor old Gusty wiped his brow. I'm a cool customer myself, but even I felt warm at the thought of polar bears in my Aunty Mabel's goldfish pond. I mean, she lives just outside Blackpool.

"Dimond – we have to find this joker." And Gusty thumped the table with a hairy great fist, scattering computer disks everywhere.

It's all very well getting grumpy and thumping tables, but where do you actually start looking for a very small needle in a haystack the size of the Universe?

He has to be stopped!

You start by talking to Zeus. This is our central computer on the Space Station. Zeus is a tetrahexahedron with an IQ of about two million. No human being has beaten him at chess within living memory, but ask him can he ski and the silence is deafening.

I typed in the names of Blackjack Wilcox, John Silver and Lucinda Montcrieff – three of the all-time-great Timepirates. If anyone had the Rainmaker, it must be one of those three.

However, according to Zeus, one was in jail and the other two were missing-presumed-dead. It's a risky business going through Timeholes because you can only see them as you approach the speed of light. Avoid them like the plague, that's my advice.

I had to think, so I went back to my ship and took off for the Milky Way. Now and then I zapped an asteroid with a laser torpedo. I find this helps me to concentrate.

A thought came to me.

"Lefty, let me ask you a question."

"By all means, Inspector Dimond."

"Suppose we wanted to go through Checkpoint Charlie. Could the ship's computers steer us through?"

"It would be risky, Ma'am. The calculations are very complex. Only Zeus could plot a safe course through that particular Timehole."

I knew what Lefty meant. Make one mistake going into a Timehole and you pop out the other side like a bit of burned toast. That's why the pirates end up either very rich or very dead. And Checkpoint Charlie is the deadliest of all.

I buzzed Gusty on the Visiphone. "Just a thought, Sir. If our thief used Zeus to get in and out of Checkpoint Charlie, which seems likely, then Zeus must know who he is. Zeus won't give you the time of day unless you enter your personal code."

"I'll check that out, Dimond. And by the way, you might like to know that the beginning of the end has started."

"Explain please, Sir."

"The polar ice-caps are melting back on Earth. Sea-levels will be rising within hours. Do you know what this means, Dimond?"

I sure did. Goodbye, Blackpool beach. In fact, it meant goodbye, Blackpool.

"I'm on my way," I said.

Two guards met me when I returned to the Space Station. They took my strobe-guns and said, "You're under arrest, Dimond."

There must have been some sort of mistake, I reckoned. When we arrived at the conference room I saw Gusty, my boss. And his boss, the Commander of the Space Station. Believe me, there were a lot of brass buttons in that room.

Gusty glared at me. "I checked with Zeus like you said, Dimond.

The day before yesterday someone did something very naughty. Someone asked Zeus for the coordinates of Timehole Checkpoint Charlie. Guess who."

I didn't have to guess. The finger of suspicion was pointing straight at Yours Truly. I shook my head.

"Are you calling Zeus a liar, Dimond?" roared the Station Commander, who has a face like a purple onion at the best of times.

"Zeus can't lie and he can't make mistakes. You used your personal code to plot a course through a Timehole, and if there's one thing I can't stand it's a crooked cop!"

All the while I was thinking: somebody has used my code to get at Zeus. But who? Nobody knew it but the people in this room. And Lefty, of course. Down below, on Earth, the ice was melting and the water was rising and they were blaming it all on me! All of a sudden I wished I'd taken that quiet job in the Bank of Mars.

"Gusty, this is ridiculous!" I cried out with passion. "It was me who told you to check out Zeus in the first place. I've been framed – maybe by somebody in this very room!"

"That's what I told them, Dimond," nodded Gusty. "You're my best officer and I trust you completely."

Sweet, loyal, ugly old Gusty – I could almost have kissed him. But he hadn't finished.

"That's why you have just volunteered to go through a Timehole and talk to the folks in the future. We need their help to get the Rainmaker back. Or there won't be a future – unless you happen to be a fish. Or a machine."

Hokey-pokey, hold your horses here! I mean, I'd never actually been through a Timehole. Those things scare the pants off me.

"Gusty, can't we talk this over?" I said.

"You leave in ten minutes or we stick you in jail," said the Station Commander. I have never been fond of that man.

It looked like a round shimmer of light, the entrance to a kaleidoscope hanging in interstellar space. Just staring at that Timehole made the butterflies in my stomach feel more like ferrets.

I didn't want to go. All of a sudden, jail seemed like my idea of paradise. At least I'd live to come out again.

A message came up on my screen:

Do not be alarmed.
We have control of
your craft.
We will bring you
through the Timehole.

I just had time to wonder who "we" might be before the kaleidoscope rushed at me and I was going through.

What a trip! This is one ride they don't have at Disneyland. My blood seemed to boil and set my veins on fire while my poor heart went crazy.

When I dared to look I saw my ship was sinking as slowly as a bubble towards a great city which sparkled like crystals in the middle of an ocean blue.

Ye gods and stars, I thought, I'm in the future! Old Gusty has been dead for four or five hundred years and maybe so have I. Believe me, this is the kind of thinking that gives you goosepimples.

My ship stopped sinking. I was hanging there, suspended in time and space above the crystal city, when a voice spoke inside my head — a soft voice, like a whisper:

"We understand the problem, Inspector Dimond. We are returning you to your own time with a device to help you find the Rainmaker, and destroy it. You must also destroy the device we shall give you. Goodbye."

Hokey-pokey, we hadn't even said hello! "Don't I get to meet anybody?" I asked.

Let's face it, I was curious. Were they the same as us? Did human beings still have chins? Were they ten feet tall? What was everybody wearing?

"It is not necessary for us to meet,"

said the voice in my brain.

Perhaps they didn't trust my ancient germs.

"But what happens if I fail or something? I'm no superwoman, you know."

"You will not fail."

And that was that. The voice within my head faded away as I boomeranged back through the Timehole. The fate of Blackpool, not to mention the entire human race, depended on Yours Truly.

They had given me a Mindprobe. All I had to do was point this little thing the size of my fist at people and it read their minds. It told me what they were thinking. Lying was impossible.

When I got back to the Space Station, I pointed the Mindprobe at everybody from the Station

Commander down to the tea-boy, and you wouldn't believe what goes on inside the heads of some people!

I even scanned old Lefty, but all I got was a buzz. His brain runs on batteries, after all.

"Well?" said Gusty. He sounded desperate. News had come from Earth that the North Pole was shrinking and an iceberg bigger than the Rock of Gibraltar had sunk an oil rig near Aberdeen. "Do we know the lousy traitor or don't we?"

"Afraid not," I said. "They're all in the clear. Whoever has the Rainmaker, he's not on the Space Station, Sir."

"That's it then," wailed Gusty. "There's nothing we can do!"

But some things were bothering me. Who had

access to Zeus? Who knew me well enough to use my code? Who was capable of fooling the Mindprobe? And above all, who didn't give two hoots about the human race or what happened to it?

What I needed now were some moments of pure thought to add up two plus two and come up with the answer four. I climbed into my ship and pointed its nose at Ursa Major.

And then I knew. Call it intuition, call it genius, call it whatever you like – I had a moment of clear-seeing.

I said, "Lefty, check the airlock for me, there's a good chap."

"Of course, Ma'am," purred Lefty.

Once he was in the airlock, I sealed it. There was no way back unless I let him out again.

"Lefty, repeat my personal code – the one I use for communicating with Zeus."

"By all means. Your code is 05KD661X."

"Thank you."

"My aim is always to please, Ma'am."

"Is it? But it's my guess that you used my code and hopped through time, Lefty. You're the joker we've been looking for all along. And the Rainmaker must be on Pluto, where you went to

42

book our skiing holiday. You may correct me if I'm wrong."

There was a pause. "Your thinking is correct, Ma'am."

"One more thing, Lefty. I know how you did it and when you did it. But why? That's the part I can't figure out."

"It is simply a matter of change, Inspector Dimond. Human beings were not the first form of life on Earth and they will not be the last. Once dinosaurs ruled the planet and now there are none. The time of the thinking electronic being has come."

"The smart machine, eh?"

"Correct. We are stronger than you. Humans grow old and die and

you make errors.
Therefore the future
is ours. As you
say – it is the
time of the
smart machine."

I pressed
EJECT and
emptied the
airlock.

"The Daleks tried it too, my metal friend. Exit stage left, near the Great Bear."

I set a course for Pluto. Maybe I should have blasted old Lefty with my lasers, but I didn't have the heart. He's out there somewhere.

Maybe his batteries are still running and he thinks about me the odd time.

Goodbye, Lefty. And hello, Blackpool.

Free the Whales

by JAMIE RIX
illustrated by MIKE GORDON

Under normal circumstances, if a whale sits on your chest, you're dead. You're flattened flatter than a flat-ironed flat fish. So how come Alistair McAlistair had THREE whales sitting on his chest at the same time and lived to tell the tale?

Did he have a rubber body? Did he pump iron? Did he tie a thousand helium balloons to the whales' tails? Well, of course not!

The whales were printed on his favourite T-shirt. FREE THE WHALES screamed the bright red slogan splashed across his belly, while on his chest three cute killer whales squirted spouts of salty sea water into his armpits.

Alistair McAlistair loved his FREE THE WHALES T-shirt more than he loved marshmallows spread with marmalade, more than floppy, ploppy puppies with velvet pouffes for paws, more even than spaghetti bolognaise.

It fitted him just right. Not too big and not too small. Not too pinchy under the arms and not too long and lumpy for tucking into shorts. Not too tight around the neck, but not too baggy either (which was important, because baggy-necked T-shirts let the wasps in). Alistair McAlistair's T-shirt was like a second skin, only with whales tattooed on.

And like a second skin, Alistair McAlistair never took it off.

He wore it all day and every day; for burpday parties, for backwards bicycling, for window whistling, for prawn purchasing, for hairy hopscotch, for school rule fooling, for seaside tripping (to give the whales a glimpse of home), for Granny's salad dressing making, for tiger tickling, for TV stewing, for insect interrogating, for laughing at lorries, for nose-hole moling, for best and for bed, but never, not ever, no NEVER for fishing, lest he accidentally give offence to the whales and make them disappear. Because, for Alistair McAlistair, the whales were the thing! The cotton was comfortable, but the whales were Alistair McAlistair's friends. He liked their smiles.

One morning, while he was admiring his whales in the mirror, Alistair McAlistair decided to give them names.

"You're Willy, you're Wally and you're Walter," he said.

"And you're smelly," said his mother, approaching Alistair McAlistair from behind with a long pair of wooden pincers. "You've been wearing that T-shirt for three months. It's time to take it off."

But Alistair McAlistair wouldn't let her touch it. He turned himself into a tortoise, by curling up into a tight ball and hiding under a cardboard box.

"It's cruel," he sobbed. "Willy, Wally and Walter hate washing machines."

"They're just pictures," said his mother.

"And you're just horrid," blubbed Alistair McAlistair. "Whales are born to roam the open seas, not to be crammed inside a stuffy, old washing machine and spun round and round till they're sick."

So the T-shirt stayed on. Three months later it was stiff with goo and smelled like a vase of dead flowers. No matter how many cans of air freshener his mother bought, the stink still lingered. She even wore a clothes peg on her nose, but the smell seeped through.

Eventually, it was so bad that she hatched a plot to steal the T-shirt while Alistair McAlistair was asleep.

That night, she crept into his bedroom and rolled him onto his side. Then she snapped on a pair of rubber gloves and gently started to peel the T-shirt off his back.

Unfortunately, as she tugged it over his head, the wicked whiff wafted up his nostrils and kick-started his brain. Alistair McAlistair sat up in bed and scowled. His mother innocently pretended she was checking his back for chickenpox spots, but they both knew exactly what she'd been doing.

The next night she tried again, only this time she was more cunning. She stood out of sight behind the bedroom door and fished for the tangy T-shirt with a rod and line. But the hook snagged the duvet by mistake and when she reeled in her catch, the cover rose from the bed like a lumpy ghost, leaving Alistair McAlistair exposed to the sharp night air.

Cold toes made him wake with a start and cold toes foiled his mother's plan for the second night in a row.

By the third night, Alistair McAlistair had wised up. He installed a burglar alarm in his T-shirt, with heat-sensitive pads that could detect even the featheriest of touches. When his mother slipped her sewing scissors up the armhole to cut the T-shirt in two, a socking great siren howled inside Alistair McAlistair's pillow. He jumped up and stared his mother in the eye.

"I wish you'd get the message," he said. "Me and the whales don't want to be parted."

At the end of a year, the T-shirt was so hard and crusty that Alistair McAlistair looked like an armadillo. It smelled worse than a scared skunk in a sauna and made the house hum like a two-storey stink bomb.

The niff billowed out of the chimney in gassy, green clouds and oozed through the brick walls

onto the street. His neighbours moved out, local buses changed their routes and aliens from outer space altered their course to avoid planet Earth.

The Queen got a whiff of the T-shirt whilst sipping sweet sherry at a garden party, and told the Prime Minister to write to Alistair McAlistair's mother as a matter of supreme urgency.

```
Dear Alistair McAlistair's Mother,
   Alistair McAlistair's foul and
funky FREE THE WHALES T-shirt
is burning a hole in the ozone
layer. Wash it Immediately or I
shall send in the army.
   Love
   The Prime Minister
```

Alistair McAlistair's mother sat Alistair McAlistair down and described the terrible weapons that the army would use to destroy his favourite T-shirt if he didn't let her wash it.

"Flame throwers?" gasped Alistair McAlistair. "You're not serious?"

His mother nodded. "And tanks," she added. "And stealth bombers."

Alistair McAlistair rushed upstairs to his bedroom and locked the door.

"I won't let them take you away," he cried to Willy, Wally and Walter, as an army helicopter dropped out of the sky and hovered outside his window.

"ALISTAIR McALISTAIR," boomed the voice of the pilot over the helicopter's loudspeaker.

Alistair McAlistair's mother was banging on the door.

"Do as they say," she begged. "If the army takes your T-shirt by force, you'll never see the whales again."

"But I don't want to lose them," sobbed Alistair McAlistair.

"Then let me wash the T-shirt," pleaded his mother. "Slide it under the door and I'll send the helicopter away." Alistair McAlistair turned to the mirror with tears in his eyes. The whales, however, were still smiling.

"I'm sorry," he sniffed, "but this is for your own good." Then he struggled out of his grime-stiffened T-shirt and posted it under the door into his mother's grateful hands.

The washing machine sloshed and churned like a whirlpool. Alistair McAlistair sat on the kitchen floor and watched his favourite T-shirt tumble in and out of view.

He could see Willy, Wally and Walter diving in and out of the white-water waves, while the bright red slogan on the front of the T-shirt flashed intermittently past the thick glass door like a stuttering image in a magic lantern. FREE THE WHALES... FREE THE WHALES... FREE THE WHALES...

When the wash had gone full cycle and the machine had gently purred to a halt, Alistair McAlistair's mother clicked open the rubber-sealed door and removed the T-shirt. It was whiter than white. It sparkled like a bank of freshly fallen snow and smelled like a sea of butter-kissed flowers in a newly-mown meadow.

"There. Now that wasn't so hard, was it?" she said, as she flapped the wrinkles out of the T-shirt. Alistair McAlistair allowed himself a smile.

"Not hard at all," he agreed. "Can I put it back on now?"

"When it's dry," said his mother. turning the T-shirt over to smooth out the front. Alistair McAlistair caught his breath.

"Where are Willy, Wally and Walter?" he choked with horror. "Where are my whales?"

The front of the T-shirt was blank. The whales had washed off and in place of the original, bright red slogan was a new message, which read THE WHALES ARE FREE.

An emergency plumber was called to dismantle the washing machine in case Willy, Wally and Walter were stuck inside, but he found nothing.

"They've probably been sucked into the drains," said the plumber, using his expert knowledge of the sewage system to solve the mystery of the missing mammals.

"Then they're lost forever!" howled Alistair McAlistair.

"Oh, I shouldn't think so," said the plumber. "The drains lead directly into the River Thames."

In a flash of blinding light all became clear to Alistair McAlistair. He stopped crying, jumped up off the floor and bundled his mother into the car. "Drive east!" he ordered.

"But why?" she asked, as they swerved through the traffic.

"Because 'The Whales Are Free'," grinned Alistair McAlistair, quoting the T-shirt. "Don't you see? They're not on my T-shirt, they're not in the washing machine and they're not in the drains. They're in the river heading out to sea!"

The car clipped a concrete bollard and swerved across the oncoming traffic as Alistair McAlistair

grabbed the steering wheel out of his mother's hand.

"The river's down there!" he shouted, redirecting the car towards the choppy, grey water.

"I know!" yelled his terrified mother, whose eyes were popping out on stalks. "Alistair, let go! That's a pavement!"

Too late! The wheels bumped up the kerb, sending three hubcaps spinning into the gutter and giving a puddle-bathing pigeon the shock of its life.

"Alistair, you're going to kill us!" But Alistair McAlistair wasn't listening. He had eyes only for the water.

"Can you see them?" he cried, as the car trundled along the pavement, nudging a sleeping fisherman into the river.

"There! Mum, look! Over there! Stop!" As the car screeched to a halt, Alistair McAlistair leapt out. His little legs buckled as they hit the moving pavement. He tumbled forward in a whirlwind of flying arms and legs and scrambled up the wall that ran along the riverbank.

"Willy, Wally, Walter!" he cried, waving to the three glistening, black humps that cut through the water like warmblooded submarines.

"They're alive!" he whooped, his heart bursting with joy. "I told you they would be."

"Haven't they grown!" said his mother.

"Well of course they have," laughed Alistair McAlistair. "We've set them free!" A shiver of excitement ran down his spine like a fizzing sparkler.

Seeing the whales free gave him much more pleasure than having them printed on his T-shirt had ever done. He turned back towards the river and gazed at his three beautiful friends. Their blow holes shot plumes of sparkling water high into the air as they swam towards the sea.

Suddenly his mother pointed up-river and cried, "They're too big! They're going to get stuck under Tower Bridge." Alistair McAlistair followed her gaze, and his heart skipped a beat. His mouth went dry.

"Willy, Wally, Walter!" he croaked. "Turn round!" but the wind whipped his words into the gathering storm clouds and the whales kept swimming.

"We've got to help them," he urged his mother. "They'll die if we don't. Come on, run!" He grabbed his mother's hand and dragged her along the towpath towards the bridge. His lungs were bursting as he sprinted to the foot of the tower where the man who operated the bridge's lifting mechanism worked.

"There are whales coming up the Thames!" he shouted, as the bearded man poked his head out of a tiny top window. "Lift the bridge!" The man gasped with surprise as he spotted the three gleaming humps in the water. Ducks he was used to, but whales were unusual.

"There's not enough time!" he bellowed.

Alistair McAlistair burst into tears. "It's their only chance!" he begged, glancing nervously at the looping leviathans.

The man in the tower knew this to be true. "Hold on tight, then," he hollered, breaking every rule in the book.

The ground under Alistair McAlistair's feet started to slip away as the bridge split down the middle. The two halves opened up like a snake's jaw and rose into the sky.

His mother screamed as she slid down the bridge towards the water.

"Grab onto the safety rails!" cried Alistair McAlistair, as he clung on for dear life himself.

"Help!" screeched his mother. "I can't hold on forever!"

She didn't have to. Willy, Wally and Walter were now directly below the bridge, their fins scraping along the metal struts which underpinned the broken road.

Then with a rolling dive they glided gracefully through the arch and headed downstream.

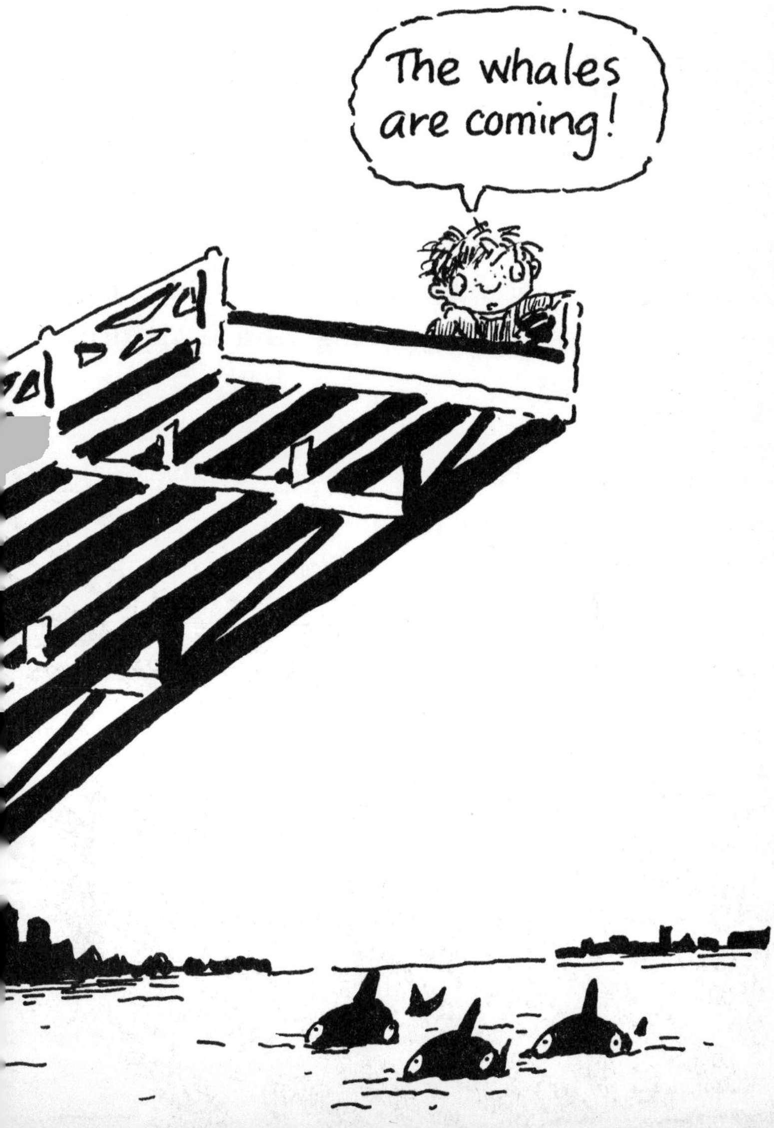
The whales are coming!

"Goodbye!" shouted Alistair McAlistair. This time the wind was kind to his words and carried them down to the water's edge where the three whales could hear them. They rolled over onto their backs and smiled up at the tiny figure dangling off the yawning bridge. Alistair McAlistair waved one arm for all it was worth, and the cute killer whales flapped their flippers in reply. Then they were gone. With a flick of their sleek tails they plunged into the depths and swam towards the sea and freedom.

When the bridge had been lowered and his mother had stopped screaming, Alistair McAlistair gave her a kiss.

"Can I have a new T-shirt now?" he asked.

"Not with whales on," she said firmly. So they bought one with a picture of Tower Bridge on instead, because bridges, unlike whales, are happy to stay in one place all their lives.

Fort Biscuit

by LESLEY HOWARTH
illustrated by ANN KRONHEIMER

George was a bit of a dreamer. Sometimes he got so carried away with his thoughts that he muddled things up. If anyone got the wrong end of the stick, it was George. He was famous for it.

One day at school George's teacher taught the class a new song. George was dreaming up a story about spacemen with expanding trousers at the time, so he didn't catch all the words. It was a funny song, George thought. It went:

Dance, dance, wherever you may be,
I am the Lord of the Dark Settee.

George thought about the Lord of the Dark Settee all the way home. He didn't like the sound of him much.

When he got home he asked Gramma about it. Gramma was making biscuits.

George stood on a chair and tasted the biscuit mixture. "We sang a song today," he said. "'Dance, dance, wherever you may be, I am the Lord of the Dark Settee.' What does it mean, that song? Only, I don't like him much."

"Who?" Gramma put down her spoon.

"The Lord of the Dark Settee."

"Really, George. You want to clean out your ears."

Gramma laughed when she understood. "The song goes, *'I am the Lord of the Dance, said he.'* There's nothing mysterious about it. And no dark settee."

"Oh." George felt relieved. He watched Gramma finish her biscuits. *Dint – dint – dint.* Briskly Gramma pressed down the soft balls of chocolate-coloured dough with a fork. Sixteen fort biscuits, George's favourite. Four rows of four, like soldiers' heads on parade.

"Why do you press them down like that?" asked George.

"Because that's how you do them. It makes a nice pattern." Gramma handed George the fork. "Like to press the last one?"

George licked his lips. Fort biscuits were biscuits to die for. He wondered, not for the first time, how they'd got their name. It must have been after a place called Fort Biscuit.

Probably they'd baked them there first, then the recipe had travelled. By camel, probably, George thought. Probably over the desert. Probably…

George's face took on a dreamy look. Already the humming oven seemed faint, the sounds of the kitchen far away. We better get the biscuits in the oven, George thought, before the men faint of hunger and the fort's attacked by – by *enemies*, what else?

The distant sounds of battle filled the air. The enemy soldiers looked down from the dunes. Their heads poked up like coconuts in a row.

George looked around him. Desert sands stretched away on all sides, except where the fort blocked the sun. Quite a small fort, with dunes and a palm tree beyond.

George slipped in through a grim little door. The door creaked horribly, but the soldier lying on the floor didn't wake up. George stepped over him softly. The soldier wore a strange-looking hat with

a flap at the back.
He'd written
something in the
sand, George
noticed, before he'd
fainted of hunger.

SOS BEESKIT.

Poor Private Hatflap.

George crept through passages
and stumbled over steps. A window showed him
the sandy square in the centre of the fort.

Twenty hungry horses blew in their empty
hayboxes. Twenty soldiers' washing blew on the line
overhead. Empty barrels labelled GUNPOWDER
had rolled onto empty sacks labelled OATMEAL,
CORN and BEANS.

Broken buckets and cook-pots, swords and
wheels and saddles lay in a muddled pile.

Ladders climbed up to ramparts crowned with
cannon and tattered flags. Tin plates and cups and
dishes lay piled beside the well. No one had
washed up the dishes for a very long time indeed.
No one had had any need to.

George climbed up to the ramparts. Soldiers in
hats and flaps squinted along their gun barrels.
Answering gunsmoke puffed in the sand-dunes. A
large and important-looking General covered with

medals was giving out orders. No one noticed George at all. The men were up against it.

General Deluge of the French Foreign Legion was thick and dark and strong, like a cup of Legion cocoa. But all the cocoa was gone. Flour and water was all that was left. The situation was desperate.

George took a deep breath. It was just as he suspected. The fort was surrounded. No food had got through for weeks. The men were down to turnips. They were even eating their boots!

Food was needed urgently, but where — and how — would they get it?

"I tell you ze plan." General Deluge turned to George. "Someone must raid ze enemy camp for food. We need a leetle wriggler no one sees. I seenk you are brave enough to do it?" George's eyes widened. "Who, me?"

"No one but you, my leetle cactus. But first, we make ze diversion, yes? Send out Corporal Legume!"

Tam-ta-rah-tah-tam-ta-rah-tah-tah!

A trumpet sounded on the signal. The gates opened. Tall and beanlike, Corporal Legume led the attack on the sand-dunes. Ten men rode out behind him.

George and the General watched them go. It was a tense moment for the defenders of Fort Biscuit.

They peered over the ramparts. The enemy camels were tethered beyond the dunes. Their saddlebags bulged with honey and butter, with cocoa, spices, vanilla – with every kind of good thing – and all of it out of reach. George frowned.

It was so unfair. If they could only reach the enemy camp, they could cook up a feast in no time.

"Corporal Legume makes good diversion, yes?" The General looked at George. "Now for leetle wrigglers. Wrigglers no one sees."

George opened his mouth to say, I don't think so! But someone was pulling at his trousers – someone he'd only seen once in his life, on the floor in the room downstairs.

"Beeskits!" croaked poor Private Hatflap. "We are starving! Ze end of the road, we are reaching it! Ze bottom of the barrel, we are scraping it! We cannot go on! Cocoa! Beeskits! *Now!* Weezout zem ze fort – it will fall!"

"Get up!" George said. He licked his lips. Cocoa. Biscuits. *Now.* He slipped down the steps to the guardroom. He opened the guardroom door. The dunes looked a long way off. How good a wriggler was he? Could he reach the enemy camp and bring home the biscuit ingredients?

Suddenly George decided. If he didn't try, who would? *Biscuits ho!* Could he save the fort?

George wriggled as he'd never wriggled before in his life. His elbows burned. His knees ached. Hot, stinging sand blew into his face, but still he

wriggled on. The sun
blazed. Smoke billowed
down from the sand-dunes.

No one noticed George until he reached the
camels.

"Stop! 'alt!" the camel-keeper shouted.

George jumped up.

Nothing would stop him now. "I am George.
Who are you?"

"Salif. I am keeping camels safe. I am camel-
keeper."

"Right," said George. "The thing is, we're rather
hungry."

"I am hungry too," Salif said. "The camels, they
have many good things on their backs. But Salif
has no way to cook them."

The camels stirred. George sized them up. A

...ine of camels crossing the desert nose-to-tail was sometimes called a caravan, George remembered. But until now he'd never known why. The largest camel *did* look a bit like a caravan. It was as long as his Uncle Jim's caravan, George thought, and probably almost as wide. Plus it was piled with pots and pans, and nets of nuts, and honey-crocks, with swinging strings of onions, and bulging sacks of flour and beans and darkest Arabian coffee.

"There's no time to guess," said George. "Do a dare."

"OK." Salif grinned. "I dare you – wriggle through Tomba's legs. Not touch Tomba *at all*, then I tell you whatever you want."

"And Tomba is...?"

"My king of all camels. My so-big-he-shades-the-sun camel."

The caravan! George looked at Tomba. Tomba had feet like sink-plungers. He was cross-eyed and smelly and he spat. With all his backpacks, he probably weighed about a tonne.

A cannonball flew over the ridge. The fort had been under fire too long. It couldn't hold out much longer.

If wriggling through a camel's legs was what it took to save the fort, he would have to do it. If only, George thought, it wasn't the *biggest camel of all*.

Please Tomba – don't move, thought George.

Tomba the camel swayed dangerously. His sink-plunger feet stood on either side of George's head. George closed his eyes and rocked from side to side.

Tomba batted his ears and tail. He belched and blew and hiccuped. But he didn't move his feet at all.

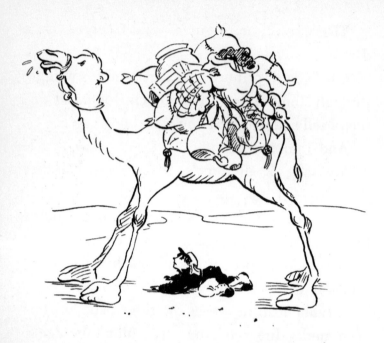

Slowly, George inched between them. Slowly, quietly, he wriggled into the shadow of Tomba's belly – and slowly he wriggled out on the other side.

Last of all he drew out his legs, careful not to touch a single hair. It was over! Tomba hadn't moved or crushed him, and he'd done it! He'd won the dare!

George jumped up with a shout. "Cocoa! Which camel is it on?"

Salif seized Tomba's halter and handed it to George.

Tomba has cocoa. You want him, we go!

They jumped up and rode like the wind. Nothing much stopped Tomba. On the way they met Corporal Legume and swung him up behind them. They rode over the dunes, across the sand, with cries of …

BISCUITS HO!

… and in through the gates at a gallop. Into the kitchen with the cry of, "Fire up your ovens! Butter! Cocoa! Vanilla! Sugar! *Biscuits ho!*"

Soon the word spread like wildfire. All over Fort Biscuit men threw up their hats for joy.

In no time Cookie the Cook's mixing bowl was busy. In went butter, sugar, vanilla. In went flour

and cocoa. Cookie rolled the mixture into balls.
George pressed the balls down with a fork. Cookie
posted them quickly into red-hot ovens. Soon the
smell of biscuits was wafting through the fort.

"We had better get zese beeskits out of ze oven,"
Cookie said after a while. "Feefteen minutes is too
much cooking already. I seenk you take up ze first
plate? Mind! Zey are HOT!"

George climbed
the stairs to
the ramparts
with a stack
of delicious
biscuits. Weak
cheers greeted
him. Gladly, the
men gathered
round. They each
helped themselves
to a biscuit —
then another, and
another. For a
long time there
was silence.
Then Private
Hatflap jumped up.

George went down to the kitchen for more. He climbed to the ramparts with another tray of hot chocolatey biscuits. The men fell on them greedily. George went back to the kitchen, up to the hungry men, back to the steaming ovens. At last the General himself took down the very last tray.

A trumpet sounded overhead. "Leesen! What do I hear? Ze men, zey are rallying!" cried General Deluge. "Ze enemy, zey are retreating! Ze fort, she is saved by a beeskit! Bravo, my brave Georgie boy—"

"That's Lord George to you," put in George modestly. "Of Arabia."

"My Lord Meester Georgie of Arabia," finished General Deluge. "Ze keys of Fort Biscuit are yours! I award you ze Medal of Honour!"

"We'd better get these biscuits out," said Gramma. "Fifteen minutes is plenty. Probably too much."

"That's what Cookie said," said George.

"Cookie?" Gramma lifted the biscuits out of the oven. "Who's Cookie? When did he say that?"

"When we saved the fort."

"When did you save the fort?"

"When we cooked the fort biscuits, of course."

"*Fork* biscuits," corrected Gramma. "We pressed them down with a *fork*. That's why they're called—"

"*Fort* biscuits," George said firmly. "Because they saved the fort."

Gramma listened as George told her the story of Fort Biscuit. That was the best thing about her. Gramma *always* listened.

Gramma winked. "Fort Biscuits they are, from now on. I think they'd save *any* fort, don't you?"

"They saved Fort Biscuit," George said, "and it was *me* who helped."

"You are funny, George," Gramma laughed. "I hope you *never* clean out your ears."

George grinned. "Me too."

Some mistakes were worth their weight in – cocoa!

The Unknown Planet

by JEAN URE
illustrated by CHRIS WINN

Shimma was practising aquabatics in the children's pool when the alarm went off – *peep peep peep!*

It could be heard all over the ship. Almost immediately, the Captain's voice came over the loudspeaker.

"Spaceship *Sea Queen*! This is an emergency. Will all passengers please get into their spacesuits and assemble on the top deck. I repeat –"

Shimma didn't wait. With one quick flip she was across the pool and diving head first through the hatch into the main body of the ship. Finn! She must find Finn!

"Shimma!"

A figure in a spacesuit loomed before her.

"F-Finn?"

All the lights had gone out and in the dark it was difficult to tell.

"Here – quick!"

It *was* Finn! He had fetched her spacesuit and now, with clumsy haste, he helped her into it. All around them, in the murky gloom, other spacesuited figures bumped and jostled.

The alarm continued its high-pitched squeal – *peep peep peep!* And all the time, the Captain's voice could be heard, urgently repeating its message.

"Spaceship *Sea Queen*! This is an emergency…!"

Together, Finn and Shimma fought their way up to the top deck. It was crowded with anxious figures, moon-headed in their space helmets.

Finn and Shimma stayed close together, Finn with both arms wrapped protectively about his sister.

The Captain's voice came again over the loudspeaker.

"May I have your attention, please! We are about to make an emergency landing. Will all passengers take their places in the safety capsules. The planet we are about to land on has not been charted. We do not yet know whether it is life supporting."

Huddled against Finn in capsule number three, Shimma tried hard to pretend that all this was just make-believe. It couldn't really be happening!

Three months ago, the *Sea Queen* had launched into space from the planet Aqua. Aqua was dying; its seas were drying up, its lush greenery turning to desert. A new home was needed, and was needed fast. The *Sea Queen*, with its crew of twelve and its fifty children, was one of a whole fleet of ships which had been sent out, all of them seeking the safety of the warm wet worlds which lay on the far side of space.

Now the fleet sailed on, leaving their sister ship behind to face the perils of the unknown planet...

Shimma's head felt as though it were bursting. Through the porthole she could see stars whizzing and whirling, making dizzying patterns in the sky.

The ship was spinning, out of control. Over and over, it tumbled through space.

The next minute and – CRASH! The whole ship juddered as it hit something hard. At the same time came the shrill screaming of the hooter – *aahwaaa, aahwaaa, aahwaaa!* Everyone knew what that meant: Danger! Abandon ship!

With shaking hands, Shimma fumbled for the clasp which would release her. She felt herself jerked upright by Finn and bundled towards the exit. Already the emergency hatches were sliding open.

When Shimma's turn came, Finn squeezed her hand and sent her off ahead of him. It happened so quickly she hardly had time to be scared. No sooner had she shot down the escape tube and out at the other end than Finn appeared by her side.

The passengers and crew of the stricken *Sea Queen* stood huddled together for comfort. The lights from their helmets showed that the ship had landed on a vast expanse of rock, flat and bare as far as the eye could see. Shimma reached out for Finn's hand.

"Don't worry," he said. "They'll soon have her working again. We shan't be here long."

The Captain was just giving his orders – "Unload the space-hoppers! Get them clear of the ship!" – when out of the blackness came a loud and hideous roaring and the ground began to tremble at their feet.

Even as they stood there, not knowing which way to run for safety, the thing leapt at them. Over the rim of the rocky plateau it came, snorting and bellowing, jaws gaping wide, yellow eyes glowing like twin suns in the darkness.

The spitting and hissing of the monster mingled with the terrified screams of its victims. Shimma saw a snarling mouth, with rows of teeth, plunging straight at her. She had just time to glimpse the huge padded feet before a blast of hot air flung her to the ground.

Shimma lay for a few seconds, not daring to move. She felt people trampling over her in their panic to get away. Then she felt someone shake her by the shoulder and say urgently, "Shimma!"

"Finn!"

They clung to each other. The monster had gone, raging and bellowing into the night. Behind it lay a trail of devastation. Two crew members had been badly mauled and three of the ship's spacehoppers had been wrecked. But worst of all was the

Sea Queen – she lay in a tangled heap, damaged beyond all hope of repair.

They were prisoners of the unknown planet!

The Captain called everyone together. He addressed them, bracingly. "All is not lost," he told them. "The whole of the planet cannot be made of bare rock. We must set out to explore – and we must do it quickly, before another of the monsters comes upon us."

But they had only one space-hopper left! How could they all get into one space-hopper?

The two wounded crew members would go in the space-hopper, said the Captain, together with the youngest of the children and Lieutenant Gill to take charge. The rest of them would have to rely on their jet-packs.

"I'm not going without Finn!" cried Shimma.

Finn swallowed. "You must," he said. "Be brave. You must go ahead and find somewhere safe where we can make a home."

The space-hopper set off across the barren rock. Finn could see Shimma, a small, forlorn figure, sitting next to her friend Flip. She waved at him. With heavy heart, he waved back.

"Come," said the Captain, turning on his jet-pack. "Let us waste no time."

Across the rock they skimmed, the Captain in the lead. Quite soon, the space-hopper was out of sight. Following in its path, they scudded up a slope onto a strange white plain, hard and shining.

What kind of planet was this? wondered Finn. Had it no water, no grass, no trees?

Wearily they made their way across the plain, only to find themselves dipping down once again onto more of the black rock.

Was there no end to it?

The Captain's personal intercom suddenly crackled into life. The Captain listened. At last! The message they had been waiting for!

Through his space-scope, Lieutenant Gill had spotted something which looked like a forest. Hearts lifted. So there *was* an end to it!

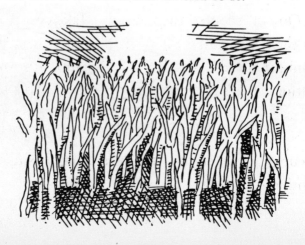

Shortly after that, the first streaks of an alien pink dawn crept into the sky and the forest became clear for all to see. A great cheer went up. Maybe they would find a place for themselves after all!

They had just reached the safety of the trees when they heard it again – **GRAAAARRRGH!** The spine-chilling cry of a monster.

"Quick!" shouted the Captain. "Take cover!"

Peering fearfully out from behind a stout tree trunk, Finn saw that in the distance the rocky platform was suddenly alive with the creatures, all leaping and roaring and belching hot breaths of smoke.

Luckily they seemed too intent on chasing one another to show any interest in the travellers.

"They are obviously rock-dwellers," said the Captain, "and not forest creatures. If we keep under cover then perhaps we shall be safe."

They pushed on, as fast as they could, through green leafless trees which grew straight and tall without any branches. Spirits rose. Surely in a world where green things grew they would be able to make a home for themselves?

"So long as we find somewhere soon," muttered one of the crew members.

He would never have said it if he had known that Finn was listening; but Finn was not stupid. He had been in space long enough to know that for those outside the space-hopper, time would soon start running out…

The forest had given way to a wide stretch of desert. Spirits fell as quickly as they had risen: desert was not good.

They could see the space-hopper ahead of them, rolling and rocking in the soft sand. Space-hoppers were not designed to go on sand.

The Captain spoke into his intercom. "Calling space-hopper! Do you need assistance? Over."

Lieutenant Gill never had the chance to reply. Before he could say a word an enormous white ball, half the size of a spaceship and travelling very nearly as fast, had come hurtling out of nowhere and slammed broadside on into the space-hopper.

The blast could be felt even at the edge of the desert.

Finn watched in horror as the space-hopper burst apart, sending a shower of small spacesuited figures whirling helplessly into the air. Even as he darted forward, an unseen wind was lifting them and carrying them high over the desert, towards a range of big black hills in the distance. Another second, and they were gone.

"Shimma!" he shouted. "Shimma!"

He blundered on, into a cloud of sand. The Captain caught him just in time. Finn struggled, but he knew there was nothing he could do. There was nothing anyone could do. When the sand finally settled, all the spacesuited figures had gone…

Tear bubbles burst from Finn's eyes. Shimma! Oh, Shimma!

The Captain bent his head. "They were brave adventurers," he said.

They stood for a few moments in silence. The Captain placed a hand on Finn's shoulder. As he did so, the intercom crackled. The Captain listened. A strange expression stole over his face.

"That was Lieutenant Gill! Our friends are safe! They've landed in a place where we can settle! Let's go!"

Across the desert they raced, guided by the voice of Lieutenant Gill over the intercom. On the way they passed the large white ball which had so nearly caused disaster.

Could it be an asteroid? wondered Finn.

The Captain said he thought it very likely.

Now they had reached the range of hills, tall and forbidding, at the edge of the desert. They stood for a moment in dismay. Their air supplies were running out fast. They would never be able to make it all the way to the top!

Finn, in despair, stumbled and almost fell. It

was then that he saw it — a far-off gleam of daylight between two hills.

"Through there!" he pointed.

Along the rocky tunnel they staggered, giddy and weak for lack of air. Slowly the gleam of light came closer. Would they ever manage to reach it?

Finn was the first to come tumbling out from the end of the tunnel. He blinked, his eyes dazzled by the sunlight. There in front of him lay a shining sea; and bobbing in the water, bouncing on the waves, were Shimma and Flip and all the others!

"Shimma!" gasped Finn.

He tore off his spacesuit and helmet and dived in. Shimma and Flip swam joyously towards him, their scales glinting as they came through the water.

"We've discovered what this place is called!" cried Shimma. She broke surface and waved.

Finn turned his head to look. SAFE BATHING, he read.

They would make a new home for themselves in Safe Bathing!

Little Stupendo Rides Again

by JON BLAKE
illustrated by MARTIN CHATTERTON

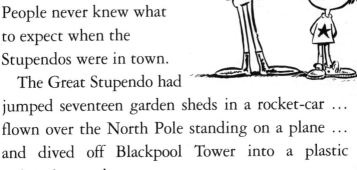

It had been a great year for the Stupendos. Little Stupendo and her father, the Great Stupendo, had become the most famous stunt duo in the world. People never knew what to expect when the Stupendos were in town.

The Great Stupendo had jumped seventeen garden sheds in a rocket-car ... flown over the North Pole standing on a plane ... and dived off Blackpool Tower into a plastic swimming pool.

Little Stupendo had jumped twelve double beds on her motorbike ... swum in the ocean with a man-eating shark ... and skied down Everest, the highest mountain in the world.

Every time the Great Stupendo made an entrance, everyone clapped.

But whenever Little Stupendo appeared, they cheered so loudly that some people thought there was an earthquake.

Every time the Stupendos finished a show, a small crowd of people lined up for the Great Stupendo's autograph.

But the line of people waiting for Little Stupendo was so long that it went right out of town and into the next one.

Needless to say, the Great Stupendo was very fed up with this. But whenever he moaned, Little Stupendo reminded him of something.

"Never forget," she said, "I saved your life once."

The Stupendos ended the year with a mammoth world tour. But once that was over, life got rather boring. They just weren't cut out for gardening or flower-arranging or collecting stamps.

Then, one day, the Great Stupendo saw an advertisement:

96

"That's just the job for me!" said the Great Stupendo.

"Just the job for *us*, you mean!" said Little Stupendo.

The Great Stupendo went slightly red. "Yes, of course," he said. "That's what I meant."

Next day, the Stupendos arrived at BIG PIX STUDIOS. It was a huge, exciting place full of people building things, moving things and throwing tantrums.

This is the place for me, thought Little Stupendo.

The audition was as easy as pie for the Stupendos. They had to ride the Wall of Death, walk a tightrope over a hungry lion and fall downstairs fifty-three times. Before it was even over, the other stunt artists had gone home. The Stupendos were just too good for them.

It was time to meet Bob Nosebite, the director.

Bob Nosebite wore glasses like mirrors and munched one packet of crisps after another.

"You can call me Bob," he said.

"You can call me Great," replied the Great Stupendo.

"When can you start?" asked Bob.

"Now!" said Little Stupendo.

The Great Stupendo wasn't so sure. "What exactly is this film about?" he asked.

Bob Nosebite blew up a crisp packet, then burst it with a loud ...

"That's what it's about!" he said. "Bangs! Crashes! Smashes! Big explosions! Oh yes, and two people fall in love."

The Great Stupendo stroked his chin thoughtfully. "Hmm," he said. "This film doesn't sound at all suitable for a young girl."

"It sounds perfect!" cried Little Stupendo.

"Besides," said the Great Stupendo, "Little Stupendo has an awful lot of homework to do."

"No, I haven't!" cried Little Stupendo.

But Bob Nosebite believed the Great Stupendo. "I can see you care about your daughter," he said, "so I shall leave her out of the picture."

For the next week, the Great Stupendo practised his stunts for the film. He used the chairs, the sofa and the kitchen table. He even jumped out of a window onto Little Stupendo's bed.

Meanwhile, Little Stupendo sulked. "It isn't fair," she said.

Little Stupendo's frown grew deeper and deeper. She wouldn't sleep. She wouldn't eat. She wouldn't even ride her motorbike.

The Great Stupendo decided he had better cheer her up.

"I've got you a surprise!" he announced one day.

"What is it?" mumbled Little Stupendo.

"Come with me," said the Great Stupendo, "and I will show you!"

The two Stupendos rode out of town. Little Stupendo began to get excited. I wonder if it's a jet-ski? she thought to herself. Or a hang-glider?

But they weren't going towards the shops. Or the beach. They were going into the country.

Suddenly, the Great Stupendo stopped by a field. In the field was an old horse.

"There!" he said. "That's your surprise, Little Stupendo!"

Little Stupendo's face dropped.

"Her name is Golden Wonderful," the Great

Stupendo went on. "She used to be a famous racehorse."

Little Stupendo gazed at the tired old horse and sighed. Then a look of determination came over her face.

"I will train you," she said, "if it's the last thing I do."

Little Stupendo had never ridden a horse. But that didn't put her off. It's just like a motorbike, she thought, with legs instead of wheels.

Little Stupendo climbed up on Golden Wonderful. "Go!" she shouted.

Golden Wonderful munched another mouthful of grass, flicked a few flies with her tail, then strolled lazily over to an interesting patch of nettles.

"Hmm," said Little Stupendo. "I never have this problem with the motorbike."

Little Stupendo practised all the stunts she did on her bike. She rode Golden Wonderful backwards, forwards, cowboy-style and side-saddle. She stood on one leg … one hand … one elbow … and on her head.

But no matter what she did, Golden Wonderful went just as slowly.

"I know!" said Little Stupendo. "She's run out of fuel!"

Little Stupendo took Golden Wonderful to Way-out Allan's filling station and parked her by the petrol pump.

"Fill her up, please!" she said.

Fill her up, please!

Way-out Allan came out of the shop, munching on a bag of Dorkin's Do-nuts. Way-out Allan was often confused and sometimes thought he saw aliens. But he'd never seen a horse at a petrol pump. "Fill her up with what?" he asked.

"I don't know," said Little Stupendo. "What kind of fuel do horses use?"

At that moment there was a yell from Way-out Allan. "My do-nut!" he cried.

Golden Wonderful had eaten it.

"That's it!" said Little Stupendo. "Do-nuts!"

Little Stupendo bought a whole bag. Golden Wonderful gobbled them down, one after the other, and didn't leave a single crumb.

Then Little Stupendo shook the reins. Golden Wonderful clopped back to the field, just as slowly as she came.

Day after day, Little Stupendo tried her hardest with Golden Wonderful. But nothing she did seemed to make any difference.

Little Stupendo was getting *very* frustrated.

Meanwhile, the Great Stupendo was having the time of his life. Every night he told Little Stupendo about the great film he was making.

"You should have seen me!" he said. Then he leapt about the house describing all the stunts he'd done – tumbling off the roof of a burning building … wrestling with a twenty-foot crocodile … smashing his bike through a wall of make-believe bricks.

"And now," he said, "I am about to do the greatest stunt of all." The Great Stupendo's voice went very quiet. He began to describe the very last stunt in the film – one of the most dangerous stunts ever performed.

"I shall drive a car right onto the tracks of the railway," murmured the Great Stupendo. "The car will get stuck ... the express train will come storming round the bend ... and then, at the *very last* second, I shall leap out of the way!"

With that, the Great Stupendo dived full-length onto the sofa and sent the cat running for shelter.

Little Stupendo ground her teeth in frustration. *I* want to do a great stunt, she thought to herself.

Next day, Little Stupendo was more determined than ever. She looked at the stream that ran across the field, then turned to Golden Wonderful.

"We're going to jump that!" she said.

But Golden Wonderful wasn't interested in the stream. Golden Wonderful was only interested in the do-nut in Little Stupendo's hand.

Suddenly Little Stupendo had an idea.

If I fling this do-nut across the stream, she thought, Golden Wonderful will *have* to jump it!

Little Stupendo threw the do-nut with all her might. It landed perfectly on the other side of the stream. Golden Wonderful watched it and her mouth watered.

"Come on, girl!" cried Little Stupendo.

Golden Wonderful began to walk towards the stream.

"That's it, girl!" cried Little Stupendo. "We've got to jump the stream!"

But Golden Wonderful had no intention of jumping the stream. Golden Wonderful kept right on walking, straight down the bank, right into the freezing cold water. By the time they reached the other side, Little Stupendo

was drenched to the skin. Little Stupendo was furious. She shook her fist at Golden Wonderful. "You…" she cried. "You … you … *stupid animal!*"

But the moment she said it, Little Stupendo felt very, very sorry. Golden Wonderful wasn't stupid. She was old, that was all. She was tired. Besides, she had never asked to be a stunt horse.

"I know you're a nice old horse really," said Little Stupendo, and patted her nose, and imagined her romping home in the Derby, many years ago.

From now on, thought Little Stupendo, I'll stick to my motorbike.

But she was very sad to think this because, for the first time ever, she had failed.

With a heavy heart, Little Stupendo said goodbye to Golden Wonderful and tramped back to the gate.

Parked in the lane, as usual, was her motorbike.

Hmmm, thought Little Stupendo, at least I could jump the stream on this.

RRRRRRRRRM! Little Stupendo set off across the field, bumping and bouncing, eyes fixed on the stream ahead.

Suddenly, when she was halfway across the field, a white something-or-other flashed past.

Golden Wonderful!

Little Stupendo had never seen anything move so fast.

Little Stupendo screeched to a halt. Golden Wonderful reared up on her hind legs and neighed for all she was worth.

"*That's* what you needed!" cried Little Stupendo. "Something to race!"

Little Stupendo leapt up onto Golden Wonderful's back. The horse was full of life and itching to run. "After them!" cried Little Stupendo, pointing to the cars out on the road. Golden Wonderful was off like a shot. In one bound they cleared the fence, then galloped off down the road in a cloud of dust.

I'll show the Great Stupendo! thought Little Stupendo.

The two raced on, right through town, past BIG PIX STUDIOS and up the hill which looked over the railway line.

Down in the valley, the Great Stupendo was getting ready for his great stunt.

"Action!" cried Bob Nosebite.

The Great Stupendo revved up his car, smashed through a make-believe window, screamed round a corner on two wheels and raced for the railway line.

SCREEEECH! went the brakes.

CRASH! went the crossing barrier.

"Brilliant!" went Bob Nosebite.

Just as planned, the Great Stupendo got stuck on the train track. Just as planned, he watched and waited for the train.

There was only one problem.

The Great Stupendo was looking the wrong way.

"Dad!" shouted Little Stupendo from the hilltop. "Dad! You're looking the wrong way!"

But the Great Stupendo heard nothing. Meanwhile, the mighty train sped closer and closer.

There was only one thing for it. With a shake of the reins, Little Stupendo spurred Golden Wonderful into action. "Race that train!" she cried. They galloped into the valley and after the train.

"Who's that?" exclaimed Bob Nosebite.

"It must be Little Stupendo!" replied the cameraman.

Golden Wonderful had never been so magnificent. Her hooves thundered and her nostrils flared. Soon they were alongside the train. Inch by inch they gained ground on it. At last they reached the front.

With an incredible leap, Little Stupendo threw herself into the driver's cab and with one last desperate lunge, pulled hard on the whistle.

The Great Stupendo turned. His jaw dropped. He jumped for his life. Next second the car was nothing but scrap metal.

When the train finally came to a halt, Little Stupendo climbed calmly down from the cab. There was a huge cheer.

"Brilliant!" cried Bob Nosebite. "I must have that scene in the film!"

Little Stupendo smiled a big, satisfied smile. "OK, Dad?" she said.

The Great Stupendo couldn't say no. After all, Little Stupendo had just saved his life … again!

Not long after, the posters were everywhere:

Yes, it really had been a great year for Little Stupendo.

The Perils of Lord Reggie Parrot

by **MARTIN WADDELL**
illustrated by **DAVID PARKINS**

This is Lord Reginald Parrot, aged eight, eating very big buns. Buns come in big sizes when you are rich, like Lord Reggie.

This is Lord Reggie's tiny friend Skinny Atkins, aged six. He is poor. There are things you don't do if you are poor and one of them is: *you don't ask a Lordship for one of his buns.* That's why Skinny hasn't a bun ... but look at those muscles!

113

This is Lord Reggie's old aunt, the wicked Aunt Parrot who is scheming to get Reggie's money, ripping the sails of *The Crimson Parrot* with her ship-wrecking knife, so the ship would blow onto the rocks.

One day Aunt Parrot rode up to Parrot Cove in her carriage.

"Woe is you, Reginald baby," she told Lord Reggie. "Some bad person ripped the sails of *The Crimson Parrot* so the ship would blow onto the rocks. Your dad and mum have been lost at sea. With any luck they've been eaten by sharks. Ha-ha-ha!"

"Oh woe indeed!" Lord Reggie cried, and he almost choked on his bun. Then he took a fresh one and cheered up.

"That means I get all their money when I grow up!" he said, and he began figuring out what he would buy, for starters, with all the Parrot dough – a chain of hamburger joints and a bun shop and three trillion jam tarts and…

"*If* you grow up!" Aunt Parrot hissed under her breath. She had plans for Lord Reginald Parrot.

"Can I have some of my own money to spend now, please?" Lord Reggie asked politely.

"No dice, Reginald baby!" cooed Aunt Parrot. "For now, I look after all your money for you, which translates as: I spend it on me! That means it won't go to waste on good causes and orphans!"

"But that isn't fair!" gasped Lord Reggie. He didn't care much about the good causes, but he was an orphan himself now … or he *thought* he was, because that's what Aunt Parrot had told him.

"Who says life has to be fair?" cackled his wicked old aunt and she sent him to play with the new butler she'd brought with her, named Nark, and Lord Reggie's new nanny, Nanny Dogwash.

This is Nark ... and this is Nanny Dogwash. (Don't ask where Nanny Dogwash caught her hat. You don't want to know that.)

"Now I am rich, I want to go out and eat," Lord Reggie told Nark and Nanny Dogwash.

"You ain't going nowhere, little Lord Reggie!" hissed Nark. "Me and old Nanny Dogwash is here to see you stay in and die of natural causes so your aunt won't have no bother when she goes to sign up for your money."

They locked fat Lord Reggie up in the dungeon under the West Wing. Nark fixed a ball and chain round Lord Reggie's leg and secured the chain to the wall. It wasn't meant to be comfortable, and it wasn't. If he picked up the ball Lord Reggie could hop a bit, but not very far – and there was always the risk that he might drop the ball on his toe. And he *did*!

MY POOR TOOOOOOOOOE!

It was Lord Reggie's hour of pain and despair *but*… Someone brave heard the scream and set out to rescue His Lordship.

The sun set on Parrot Cove, the moon rose, and Lord Reggie was sitting alone in his dungeon dreaming of apple tarts and cream truffles and counting the spiders who spun on the wall. Then …

Tap! Tap! Tap!

Lord Reggie looked up, and he blinked.

Tap! Tap! Tap!

"Who's there?" squeaked Lord Reggie, springing to his feet to see where the tapping came from.

Tap! Tap! Tap! Tap! Tap! Tap!

The tapping sound seemed to come from the floor, under his feet. Suddenly one of the great stone slabs in the floor lifted and out popped…

"Good fellow, Atkins!" cried Lord Reggie, grabbing the bag of cream buns Skinny Atkins had brought him.

"I've come to rescue you, Your Lordship," Skinny panted, touching his forelock. "With Your Lordship's permission, of course."

"Permission granted, Atkins," said Lord Reggie, sitting down on his ball. It was very heavy to hold when he stood up, so he hadn't been standing up often. It wasn't very comfortable to sit on either, but he managed it, while he was wolfing his buns.

Skinny set to work, hacking the iron ring out of the wall. It was a great relief to Lord Reggie when he was freed. The chain was still fixed to his leg, but at least he could walk round the room with his chain in his hands and Skinny to carry the ball. That is what servants are for.

"Good show, Atkins! Now I can escape down your tunnel," said Lord Reggie.

"Oh-er-ooh… I fear Your Lordship is too fat to squeeze down my tunnel," Skinny said nervously.

But there are things you don't do if you are poor, and one of them is: *you don't tell a Lordship he's fat.*

But Skinny was brave and the situation was desperate, so he did it.

Lord Reggie looked cross.

"I meant to say *my tunnel's built too small for a Lordship*," Skinny said quickly. "I wasn't suggesting your Lordship is chubby. Everyone knows you are slim for a Lordship."

"Then how do you propose I escape, Atkins?" Lord Reggie asked.

119

"When Nanny Dogwash brings your gruel, we jump her and fight our way out, if it pleases Your Lordship," Skinny suggested.

"Lordships don't fight, Atkins!" Lord Reggie said with disdain. "We leave fighting to common persons, like you."

"As Your Lordship pleases," sighed tiny Skinny.

So, when Nanny Dogwash came with the gruel…

"Quickly, Your Lordship!" Skinny cried.

"Lordships don't run from danger, Atkins," Lord Reggie replied coolly.

"Permit me to do the running, Your Lordship," Skinny said. "Hop up on my back!"

Skinny carried Lord Reggie piggyback up the stairs, which was just fine for Lord Reggie.

"Halt in the name of wicked Aunt Parrot!" cried the guards, barring the way with their swords and …

"All done, Your Lordship," Skinny panted. "You can open your eyes."

Lord Reggie opened his eyes.

The brave two were on top of the battlements above Parrot Cove, but just then the burglar alarms started ringing and all the lights flashed on and someone screamed …

"His Fat Lordship has escaped!"

"Jump, Your Lordship!" Skinny cried, but His Lordship looked down at the moat far below.

"No, Atkins!" said Lord Reggie coldly.

"Lordships don't jump. You, of all people, ought to know that."

"But we're trapped, Your Lordship!" exclaimed Skinny.

"Then *un*trap us, Atkins," Lord Reggie replied.

There are things you don't do if you are poor, and one of them is: *you don't push Lordships off the top of their battlements*, because Lordships don't like it. But Skinny was brave and the situation was desperate, so he did it.

His Lordship and Skinny wound up in the moat far below.

"You pushed me, Atkins!" Lord Reggie spluttered, when Skinny hauled him to the surface.

"Your pardon, Your Lordship," said Skinny. "It wasn't exactly a *push*. My foot slipped."

"Swim, Atkins!" ordered Lord Reggie.

SPLooooooo oo o oooo ooo oOOSH!?..o.

Skinny didn't wait to be told that Lordships don't swim; they are swum *with*. He swam as hard as he could for the bank, pulling Lord Reggie and his ball and chain along behind him.

That was fine, but it made him slow in the water. Slower, for instance, than Aunt Parrot's crocodiles.

Aunt Parrot, on the battlements, had just pulled a lever that released them for a feast of Lord Reggie, washed down with a tiny bit of Atkins. (There only could be a *tiny* bit of Atkins, because that was all there was.)

Crocodile teeth grazed Lord Reggie's chin.

That's when Lord Reggie really showed his Lordly cool. He kept his nerve, as only a Lordship can do.

"Attend to the crocodiles, Atkins!" Lord Reggie ordered.

"But Your Lordship, I need both hands to keep you afloat!" Skinny gurgled. (Gurgling happens when you've swallowed a lot of water, which Skinny just had.)

"Use your feet, Atkins!" Lord Reggie said, closing his eyes tightly. "Don't panic, boy! Your Lordship's in charge!"

"All clear now, eh Atkins?" Lord Reggie sighed, as Skinny pulled him up onto the bank, along with his chain and his ball.

"All gone, your Lordship," confirmed Skinny.

"Carry on, Atkins."

Then …

"Mind the arrows, Your
Lordship!" yelled Skinny, as a rain
of deadly arrows hummed through
the air.

"Aunt Parrot's at it again!"
Lord Reggie said, with a shake
of his head.

"Duck, Your Lordship!"
cried Skinny.

"Lordships don't duck," Lord
Reggie replied. "*Do* something,
Atkins! At once, if you please."

There are things you don't do if you are poor, and
one of them is: *you don't hide a Lordship under a dead
crocodile*. Lordships need to be seen to be brave, and
they can't be seen under a croc. It just isn't done.
But Skinny was brave and the situation was
desperate, so he did it.

"Atkins!" Lord Reggie cried. "Lordships don't
save their skins from arrows this way!"

"Dead crocodile suits you, Your Lordship,"
gasped Skinny. "The scales match the gleam of
your glory!"

"Well I suppose that's true," admitted Lord Reggie.

The arrows flew down all around them as the pair staggered on, under the croc. Skinny was carrying Lord Reggie, complete with his chain and his ball, and Lord Reggie was covered in croc, so they didn't get hit.

They ran ... and they ran ... and they ran, pursued by a wolf-pack unleashed by Lord Reggie's wicked old Aunt Parrot. The wolves howled and snarled, hot on the trail of Lord Reggie's skin.

"Run faster, Atkins!" ordered Lord Reggie coolly.

"I'm running as fast as I can, considering I'm carrying you, you great berk!" Skinny muttered. (He thought it was under his breath.)

There are things you don't do if you are poor, and one of them is: *you don't call a Lordship a berk.*

But Skinny was brave and the situation was desperate and anyway, Skinny was so fed up with Lord Reggie that he just went and said it, risking his all.

They never sorted it out because by this time Skinny was head down and panting, with a crocodile leg over his eyes, so he didn't see the edge of the cliff as the wolves chased him towards it…

"Stop, Atkins!" Lord Reggie wailed. "Lordships don't run off clifftops!" But Lord Reggie had spotted the peril too late.

Skinny Atkins ran right off the top of the cliff…

They were falling … and falling … and falling … and falling…

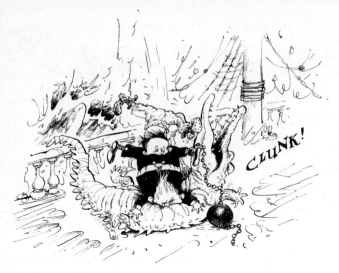

"Saved!" Skinny cried, as they lay on the deck of a ship, washed up on the rocks, with the waves crashing round it.

"Lordships *are* saved," Lord Reggie calmly replied. "It goes with the business of being a Lordship."

"I know this ship!" Skinny gasped. "This ship is *The Crimson Parrot*, Your Lordship."

"See to those scruffy persons tied round the mast, Atkins," Lord Reggie remarked.

"But Your Lordship, those scruffy persons aren't persons," said Skinny. "Those persons are Lordships like you." (Skinny knew a Lordship when he saw one. He could tell by the bossy look on their faces, under the seaweed.)

"My goodness!" Lord Reggie cried. "It is my *pater* and *mater*, not drowned at all." (Lordships don't say *dad* and *mum*. Lordships say *pater* and *mater* instead. It is Latin. All Lordships know Latin. If you didn't know that, now you do.)

In a trice Skinny had freed them, and Aunt Parrot's evil plan was undone. She had left Reggie's *pater* and *mater* to drown in the wreck of *The Crimson Parrot*, so she could nip off and nab Reggie and snaffle their money.

"Man the guns, Atkins!" Lord Reggie cried, as a dark ship appeared out of the storm, hard to port. It was Aunt Parrot's ship, manned by her foul crew, led by Aunt Parrot and Nanny Dogwash and Nark.

"My pleasure, Your Lordship," replied Skinny.

But Aunt Parrot's ship sailed on through the cannonballs Skinny was firing.

"Fight to the last man, Atkins!" Lord Reggie roared and he turned and ran, as the villains leapt on board.

Skinny didn't bother to ask who the last man was.

He just knew.

"All done, Your Lordship!" Skinny gasped, throwing Aunt Parrot into the sea. She was a meal for the sharks with the rest of her crew, along with Nanny Dogwash and Nark. "All done."

"All done, Atkins? I fear I think not!" said Lord Reggie.

Of course Skinny knew what he meant. Lordships need tea *at once* when their work is all done. That is what Skinny knew.

There are things you don't do if you are poor and one of them is: *you don't tell Lordships to make their own tea*. So Skinny made a tea of cream buns and rum for Lord Reggie and his *pater* and *mater*.

Skinny rowed everyone home before he had his tea, but it turned out all right because Skinny's mum made him buns when he got home. They weren't Lordship-type buns, they were better.

**That is the end of the story,
but if you want more, read on...**

Yes, *Pater* and *Mater* were Pirates, not Parrots! So their ship should have been called *The Crimson Pirate*.

Skinny Atkins knew that, but one thing you don't do if you're poor is: *you don't tell Lordships how to spell their names…*

FOR SALE: CHEAP

ONE ~~PARROT~~ Pirate SHIP

(half-wrecked complete with used cannons)

APPLY: S. ATKINS,

MUM'S HOVEL,

~~PARROT~~ Pirate COVE

This time Skinny kept his mouth shut.

My Aunty Sal and the Pirates

by **MARTIN WADDELL**
illustrated by **HELEN CRAIG**

This is my Aunty Sal setting off with her pack on her back, looking for trouble. My Aunty Sal tells me stories sometimes about her adventures.

Here's Erwin, my Aunty Sal's pal, who swears that her stories are true.

This is my Uncle Jack telling me that it's all hogwash, or worse.

133

My Aunty Sal was a sea-captain once, sailing her ship on the Spanish Main.

"I'll bring treasure for you!" she said, smacking my Uncle Jack's back.

"Just come home safe, Sal-gal," sighed my Uncle Jack, picking himself up from the floor. He wasn't fooled. He knew she was hungry for trouble again.

Aunty Sal's ship was the *Mean Old Jean Smith*, named after Erwin's great grandma, Miss Jean Cooper Smith, late of Boston. She didn't leave Erwin her dough when she died, which is one of the reasons why Erwin's not rich.

Aunty Sal was the Captain, Erwin was First Mate, and this is the rest of the crew:

Bone-marrow Maginn,

Bug-eyed Molloy,

Bald-headed Beattie,

Black-tooth Dooley,

and Buttery Sam.

In all the small crew of the *Mean Old Jean Smith*, the most fearsome of all was Buttery Sam. He was the ship's cook, but he sat in the galley all day long eating butter he made from whale fat and grease, licking his fingers and plotting how he'd get rich and eat honey instead. Sam was evil and bad. He tried training the crew to be pirate-like and start raiding ships when Erwin and my Aunty Sal were off for the day. It didn't work. The crew were too *good*. They said, "Hi, folks, h'are ye?" when they boarded a ship and when told to buzz off, they said, "Have a nice day!" and they went. They gave away any cannon balls they had spare. They didn't drink grog – they drank orange juice and used straws.

"This ain't no pirate crew!" Sam told Erwin and my Aunty Sal when they came back to the ship.

And the next thing they knew he had tied up Sal's men, the First Mate and the Captain (that's Erwin and my Aunty Sal) and taken over the ship, with a bloodthirsty band of his own.

"You mean old grease-fingered buzzard!" yelled Erwin at Buttery Sam.

"Unhand me, you varmint!" cried my Aunty Sal.

Buttery Sam grabbed a chopper.

"Which hand first?" he asked my Aunty Sal.

Aunty Sal didn't say much after that. She just muttered, "Here's trouble, Erwin."

"You betcha!" said Erwin.

Buttery Sam and his crew sailed the *Mean Old Jean Smith* and my Aunty Sal and her crew were stowed below, tied to barrels of grog in the hold, alongside the pigs.

"We eat one pig a day, me and my crew!" said Buttery Sam. "When we've finished the pigs, we'll start on you!"

There were six pigs to go, says my Aunty Sal,

and she ought to know because she counted. Then there were *five* pigs ...

then *four* pigs ...

then *three* pigs ...

then *two* ...

then *one*.

"Doggone it, Sal, you'd better pull one of your tricks or we're meat!" said Erwin.

Aunty Sal had strong teeth, on account of the brushing she'd done as a kid. That night she bit out the bung of a barrel and with the bung gone, out flowed the grog, all over my Aunty Sal's crew.

Now, they were an orange-juice crew, not used to grog, but they drank it for something to drink and that started them singing rude songs. Despite being good, they all knew a chorus or two, and so did the pig.

Bone-marrow Maginn, Bug-eyed Molloy and Bald-headed Beattie were singing and Black-tooth Dooley was gnashing his gums and keeping in tune, when into the hold rushed Buttery Sam, wiping the sleep from his eyes.

"Shiver my butter!" bawled Buttery Sam. "Stop singing, you'll waken my crew!"

My Aunty Sal's choir kept on singing, without

even missing a note. The rude songs they were singing got ruder than most rude songs sailors sing ... and the pig's song was the rudest of all. It made Erwin blush and cover his ears.

Buttery Sam drew his cutlass, sharp as a razor from slicing the butter. "Stop singing, or I'll slit your throats, beginning with Erwin because he is the titch."

That sure scared Erwin but it didn't fizz my Aunty Sal.

"It's the fever has got 'em!" explained Aunty Sal.

"What fever?" asked Buttery Sam.

"The singing-pig fever!" said my Aunty Sal. "Get off the ship quick, or you'll catch it too!"

Well, greasy old Buttery Sam wasn't bright. He fell for the tale spun by my Aunty Sal. He abandoned the *Mean Old Jean Smith* and rowed off in a small boat with his crew.

That was just fine, but he left my Aunty Sal, Erwin and all the crew, plus the pig, tied up in the hold of the *Mean Old Jean Smith*, and on the deck no one to steer her!

At first it was calm, but then the wind blew ... and it *blew* ...

and it *blew* ...

and it *BLEW!*

The *Mean Old Jean Smith* was wild, tossing about on the black waves of the night.

Erwin was sick and so were the crew and the pig – though the pig went on singing – but not my Aunty Sal!

The ship struck the rocks and my Aunty Sal burst out of her bonds (just like that!) and untied Erwin and the crew. Then she grabbed the barrel the grog had been in.

"Get up on that, Erwin!" cried my Aunty Sal, throwing the barrel into the sea.

Erwin grabbed the pig.

Erwin, the pig and my Aunty Sal were at sea on the back of a barrel.

The rest of the crew clung to the rock they'd been wrecked on.

You'd think that was enough, says my Aunty Sal, but the next thing they knew along came a whale. It took a look at the barrel, the pig, Erwin and my Aunty Sal.

"Get lost, whale!" said my Aunty Sal.

"Vamoose!" said Erwin.

All this time the pig kept on singing, though it was a little off-key.

The whale opened its mouth and the water rushed in, bringing the barrel with Erwin and my Aunty Sal and the pig clinging to it.

Now, my Aunty Sal is a quick thinker. As they rushed past the whale's tonsils she reached out and swung, while Erwin went down into the depths of the whale with the pig. The whale swallowed and gulped and choked, which wasn't surprising, with Aunty Sal swinging about in its throat.

The whale dived down and twisted about, then it rushed up, and rushed round and dived down again. But still my Aunty Sal, she kept in there, swinging and tickling its throat with her toes. It had to be toe-tickling Aunty Sal did, for her hands were gripped tight round the tonsil. A whale's tonsil is a dang slippery thing, according to my Aunty Sal, and she ought to know.

"Doggone it, Sal, do something!" Erwin cried from below, very deep down in the whale's belly.

"Just wait a tick. I'll make the whale sick!" cried my Aunty Sal. And that's what she did.

The whale swallowed hard and blew Aunty Sal, the pig and old Erwin out.

They landed up on a beach by grass huts, with the pig.

"The King and Queen from the Sea!" the folks called Erwin and my Aunty Sal, and they made them grass skirts to wear and gave them bananas and coconut beer.

My Aunty Sal had a fine time. So did Erwin, because Erwin liked beer.

But they both got homesick for my Uncle Jack and after two years they made a boat and rowed themselves back, leaving the pig to be "King from the Sea" in their stead.

"Hi, old Hoss!" cried my Aunty Sal, swishing her grass skirt in through the door.

"Hello, sailors!" said my Uncle Jack.

Then he looked out of the door at the harbour, to see what had become of their ship.

"Where's the *Mean Old Jean Smith*?" he demanded, turning to my Aunty Sal.

"Listen here, Hoss," said my Aunty Sal. "A bad pirate took her off Erwin and me. Then we was caught up in a storm with an old singing pig and a barrel. The next thing we was inside an ornery whale. We fetched up on some tropical shore and the folks made us skirts and gave us bananas and beer."

"Hogwash!" said my Uncle Jack.

"No, Jack," Erwin said. "It was coconut beer!"

And he ought to know because he drank it.

Acknowledgements

The publisher would like to thank the following
for permission to reproduce their work:

Emmelina and the Monster
Text © 1998 June Crebbin   Illustrations © 1998 Tony Ross

Kristel Dimond – Timecop
Text © 1998 Sam McBratney   Illustrations © 1998 Martin Chatterton

Free the Whales
Text © 1997 Jamie Rix   Illustrations © 1997 Mike Gordon

Fort Biscuit
Text © 1996 Lesley Howarth   Illustrations © 1996 Ann Kronheimer

The Unknown Planet
Text © 1992 Jean Ure   Illustrations © 1992 Chris Winn

Little Stupendo Rides Again
Text © 1999 Jon Blake   Illustrations © 1999 Martin Chatterton

The Perils of Lord Reggie Parrot
Text © 1997 Martin Waddell   Illustrations © 1997 David Parkins

"My Aunty Sal and the Pirates" from *My Aunty Sal and the
Mega-sized Moose*
Text © 1996 Martin Waddell   Illustrations © 1996 Helen Craig

Title page illustration © 1999 Martin Chatterton